For D.B.

First U.S. edition 1991   1 2 3 4 5 6 7 8 9 10

Library of Congress Cataloging in Publication Data was not available in time for publication of this
book, but can now be obtained from either the publisher or the Library of Congress.
ISBN 0-688-09872-X   ISBN 0-688-09873-8 (lib. bdg.)
LC Number: 90-6374

THE FISHERWOMAN

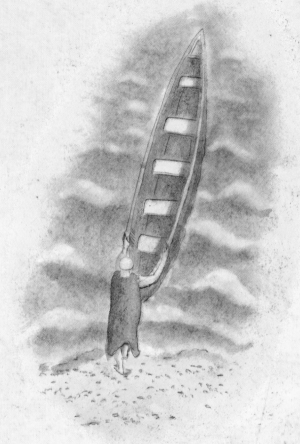

Louise Brierley

Words by

Anne Carter

LOTHROP, LEE & SHEPARD BOOKS
NEW YORK

In a small, shabby village beside the sea lived Maud, the fisherwoman. By day, she combed the shore for shells and sea wrack. As the sun set, she rowed her long, lean boat out over the water and let down her fishing net. And this was how she made her living.

But, sitting alone, while her boat rocked gently under her, Maud dreamed. Her dream was always the same: dressed in beautiful clothes, she moved among the rich and famous people who lived behind the great gates of the mansion above the village.

One night, when the time came to draw in her net, Maud felt a hard bump against the side of the boat. Her head filled with visions of sunken treasure; jewels, perhaps, worth more than a king's ransom. But when she hauled the net aboard, all she found, among the flapping bream and mackerel, was an old pink vase.

Maud took the vase home with her and
put it in her window. Now and then, as she
sat at her table, her eyes would rest on it and
fancy that they saw, on its sea-encrusted sides,
shadowy figures moving in a kind of dance.
But time passed, bringing other curious
trophies from the sea, and Maud lost
interest in the vase.

With autumn came high winds and seas too fierce for fishing. Maud lay in bed, but not asleep. Outside, the storm raged and the rain lashed her house. Soon, beneath the turmoil, came a sullen dripping. Sighing, Maud got up and began putting out every pot and jar she had to catch the water. Among them was the old pink vase. The hollow drips became a musical splashing and Maud slept.

The storm blew itself out and a red dawn gave way to quiet sunshine. Out of Maud's pink vase grew a tall rubbery stem with, at the very top, a single large pink flower bud. It was the first thing she saw when she awoke.

While she watched, the bud expanded into a wild, beautiful, shell-like flower. Maud was entranced. She moved the vase into a sunny corner and gazed at the flower for a long, long time.

She spent the rest of that day gathering shellfish off the rocks and picking up storm wreckage from the beach. When she came home, she saw that the petals of the pink flower had fallen and, in their place, as if the tree had fruited, was the most incredible pink hat.

Maud picked it. It came quite readily into her hand. She hurried to her looking glass and tried it on.

Next morning, Maud's wonder grew. The plant had borne two more fruits in the shape of a pair of marvelous pink shoes.

Maud leaped out of bed and put them on. They fitted perfectly. She wanted the whole world to see. She went out, without pausing for breakfast, parading up the village street to show off her finery. People greeted her and Maud smiled graciously but did not speak.

On the third morning, Maud woke very early. She was not disappointed. The tree had fruited again, still more magnificently. This time it bore a pink dress, the most beautiful thing that Maud had ever seen. It fitted as if it had been made for her.

Maud hurried out to show herself. She held her head so high that she did not even see the friends who greeted her. Or the grins that followed her up the street.

She was strolling along the promenade when the Contessa came by in her gondola.

"Dear madam, will you join us at my mansion? The garden party is about to begin."

And so, to the lap-lapping of the water and the chat-chatting of the lady, Maud was borne across the bay.

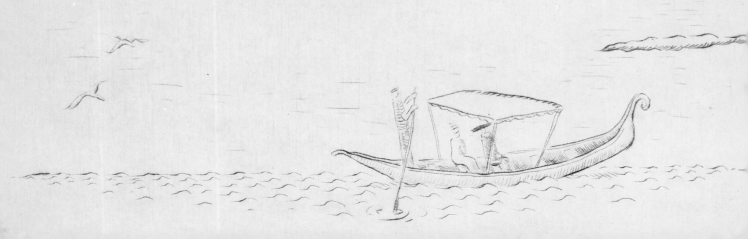

Inside the high walls, the music and the
fountains played. People talked and laughed
and such a banquet was laid out as Maud had
never in her life imagined. All day she reveled in
wealth and splendor, thinking of nothing but the
pleasure of it all. Long shadows crept across the
lawns and still the guests sat eating and drinking.

The late sun gilded the great gates and Maud could see the villagers passing by outside. A fat man sitting next to her was mocking them. Maud looked around her, saw the greedy faces, heard the heartless laughter, and suddenly she knew how selfish she had been. She did not belong here, sealed behind these iron gates. Her place was in the real world, doing the work she knew, among friends.

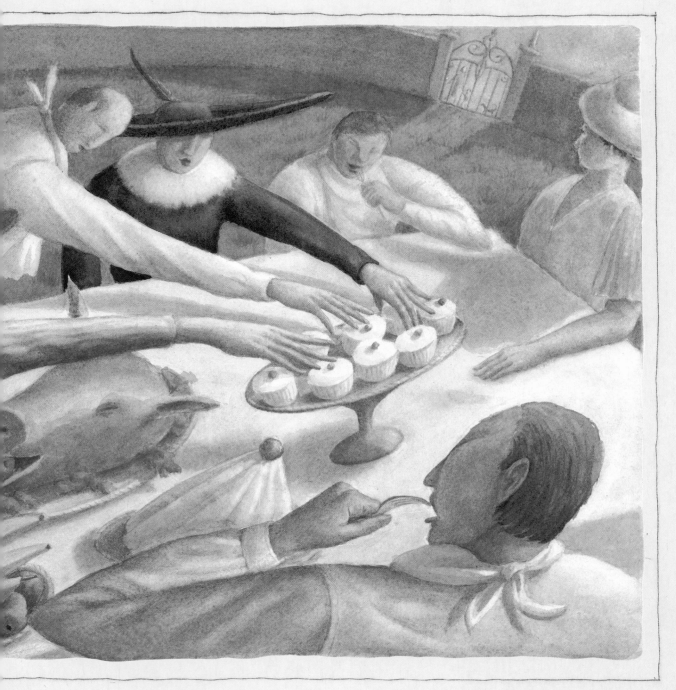

In a second, Maud had left the table. Kicking off
the pink shoes, she ran wildly over velvet lawns, past
marble statues, stately urns, and shaded monuments,
 out into the quiet streets.

The sun had set. The people were
all indoors. But still Maud did not stop. She ran
on blindly through the sheltering dark. Her glorious hat
was lost, her dress was dirty and torn. She did not think
of them. Her ears were full of mocking laughter and
her tired feet carried her without thought
the swiftest way to home.

Shame pursued her as she slammed the door
behind her. Her own house rocked and hummed with it.
And the tree in the corner stood lifeless and dead.

Maud did no fishing that night. She stripped
off the ruined dress and huddled in her bed, haunted
by nightmare banquets filled with greedy, gobbling
faces and shrieks of cruel mirth.

In the morning she rose and went down
to the shore. With her she took the remains
of the dress and the pink vase with its
withered plant.

All day Maud worked hard with her needle, and when her long lean boat put out to sea, there was a sail to drive it. The setting sun was spreading gold upon the water as she lowered her net and waited for the fish that were her livelihood. Tired but content, Maud watched the splendor fade.

But first, she dropped the pink vase overboard and let it sink.